For Lily
R.C.

For Alice and Thomas
P.H.

First published in the United States 1997 by
Dial Books for Young Readers
A Division of Penguin Books USA Inc.
375 Hudson Street
New York, New York 10014

Published in Great Britain by
Reed Children's Books
Text copyright © 1997 by Peter Harris
Pictures copyright © 1997 by Reg Cartwright
Printed in China / First Edition
1 3 5 7 9 10 8 6 4 2

Library of Congress Cataloging in Publication Data
Harris, Peter, date.
Mouse creeps / by Peter Harris ; pictures by Reg Cartwright.—1st ed.
p.   cm.
Summary: Unwittingly a mouse sets off
a series of events that end a war.
ISBN 0-8037-2183-8   [1. Mice—Fiction.   2. War—Fiction.
3. Stories in rhyme.]   I. Cartwright, Reg, ill.   II. Title.   PZ8.3.H24315Mo
1997 [E]—dc20 96-21147   CIP   AC

Mouse Creeps

by Peter Harris

pictures by Reg Cartwright

Dial Books for Young Readers

New  *York*

Dog sleeps.
Mouse creeps.

Cat sees.
Mouse flees.

Horse jumps.
Churn dumps.

Ducks wake.
Pigs escape.

Ducks fly.
Hunters spy.

Hunters shoot.
Ducks scoot.

Drums beat.

Armies meet.

Soldiers fear.
Battle near.

Drummer sighs.
Then surprise!

Acorns tumble.
General stumbles.

The other drops.
Fighting stops.

Soldiers roar.
End war.

Father at door.
Soldier no more.

Dog sleeps.
Mouse creeps.